淘气的乒乓猫

乒乓猫上报纸

〔荷〕米斯·博豪宇斯 著　　〔荷〕菲珀·维斯顿多普 绘　　蒋佳惠 译

人民文学出版社
PEOPLE'S LITERATURE PUBLISHING HOUSE

一个星期天的早晨，
乒乓正在读报纸。乓乓呢？

It's Sunday morning.
Pom is reading the newspaper. And Pim?

每当乒乓读报纸的时候，
乒乒就会觉得有些无所事事。

**Pim always feels a bit bored
when Pom is reading the newspaper.**

"你读完了吗，乒乓？"
可是，乒乓还需要一点时间把一篇文章看完。

'Have you finished yet, Pom?'
But Pom has to read out this bit.

“不……哎呀……哦哟……哈哈哈！”乒乓轻轻地笑了起来。

“报纸上都登了些什么，乒乓？”乒乒问。

'No!... gosh... oh dear... ha ha ha!' Pom chuckles.

'What's in the newspaper then Pom?' Asks Pim.

"嗯，也没什么，就是常发生的事情。"乓乓说。

"那猫咪上过报纸吗？"乒乒想要知道。

'Well just the things that happen,' says Pom.

'And do pussycats ever get in the newspaper?' Pim wants to know.

"是的，有时候。"乒乓说。

"但只在他们做出一些非常特别的事情的时候。"

'Yes, sometimes,' says Pom.

'But only if they've done something really important.'

"我也想要，乒乓！我也想要上报纸。"
"我明白，乒乓，可是，不可能平白无故上报纸的。"

'I want to be in the newspaper too, Pom!'
'Yeah but Pim, you don't get in the newspaper for nothing.'

乒乓想到了一个主意。
"我们要做什么呢，乒乓？" 乓乓问。

Pim has an idea.
'What are we going to do Pim?' Asks Pom.

"去寻找危险。
到时候，我们就可以见义勇为。"

'Search for danger.
So that we can do something heroic.'

"不可能平白无故上报纸的！
这话可是你自己说的，乒乓。"

'You don't get in the newspaper for nothing!
You said it yourself, Pom.'

"大救星来了。
嗨！那是什么？"

'Here comes the famous hero.
Hey, whatever could that be?'

"那是不是一个身陷险境的孩子？
我们最好去看看！"

'Is that a CHILD in danger??
We'd better go and see!'

"你靠边站，我这就冲上去救她！
快快把她捞到岸上！"

'Stand back and let me help her.
I'll pull her out, by golly!'

"坚持住，我眼看就要够到她。
噢不！只是一个布娃娃。"

'Hang on, I've nearly got her,
Oh no! It's just a dolly!'

"哎呀呀，这可真让人气馁。
这样的事情怎么上得了头条把牛吹：

'That won't make the headlines.
It's nothing but a ruse:

'英雄乒乒勇救落水布娃娃！！'
这可不是什么大新闻！"

"Pim saves DOLL from drowning!!"
That's not important news!'

"我是著名的作家乒乓。
我用我美丽的猫爪子，写出了这本书，把知识传递给每一位。"

'I'm Pom the famous author. I wrote this book myself.
I penned it with my own fair paw. It's flying off the shelf!'

"书里满是美丽的图片还有文字，充满猫咪的智慧。
读完您一定对我心生敬佩。"

'A book with lovely pictures and words all in a row.
It's full of feline wisdom and things that you should know.'

"只不过，你永远不会在人类的报纸上看到——

'But in the human's paper
You will never see it written——

头版上的大标题：
'猫咪写的畅销书！！'"

In big letters on the front:
BESTSELLER BY A KITTEN!!'

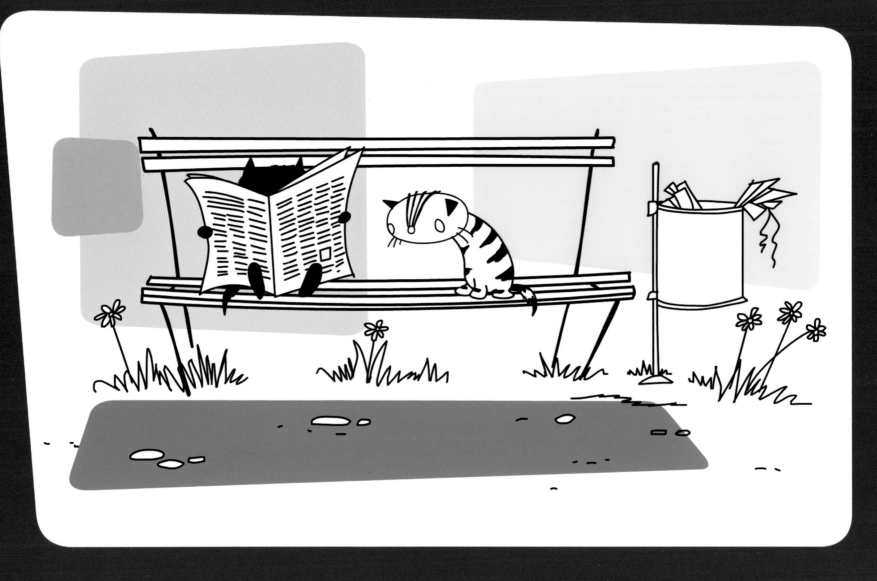

"我们怎样才能上报纸呢？
这里什么新鲜事也没有。"

'How will we ever get in the newspaper?
Nothing ever happens to us.'

等等，这是怎么一回事？

But, what is this?

"快，乒乓，跟上去！"

'Come on, Pom, after it!'

"喂，"乒乒和乓乓勇敢地说，
"你们想干什么？"

'Hey,' say Pim and Pom bravely,
'what are you doing there?'

"我们一定要抓住那只丑陋的猫。"那只凶神恶煞般的恶霸猫说道。
"她的眼睛很诡异，颜色也很奇怪。"

'We're going to get that ugly cat,' says the bully-cat.
'She's got strange eyes and with a funny colour too.'

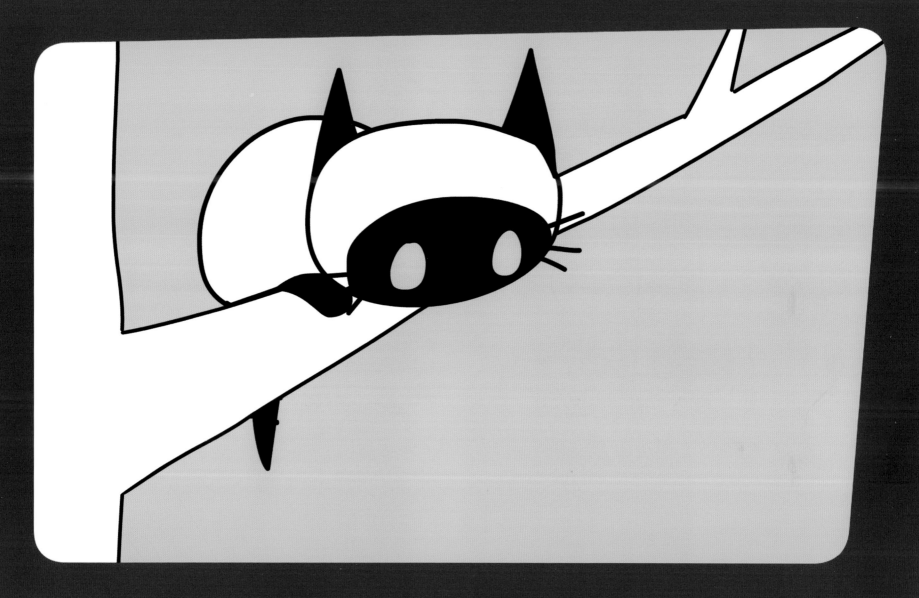

"她一点儿也不丑陋。"乓乓说。
"实际上她很漂亮呢。她的眼睛像天空一样湛蓝。我要管她叫天眼。"

'She's not ugly at all,' says Pom. 'She's actually very beautiful.
Her eyes are as blue as the sky. I'm going to call her Sky-Eyes.'

"天眼，"乒乓说，"真是个可爱的名字！"
其他猫咪也这么觉得。

'Sky-Eyes,' says Pim. 'That's lovely!'
The other cats agree...

只有那只凶神恶煞般肥肥胖胖的恶霸猫是个例外。

他咬着牙说："你们不要上当，她跟我们不一样！"

All except for the big mean bully-cat.

'Don't be fooled, she's different to us,' he hisses.

这下，乒乓真的生气了。

"走开！要不然……要不然……"

Now Pim gets really angry.

'Scram! Otherwise...otherwise...'

"要不然怎么样，你想要打架吗？"凶神恶煞般的恶霸猫咆哮道。
"我们可是二对一哦！"乒乓勇敢地说。

'Otherwise what, are you looking for a fight?' bristles the mean bully-cat.
'That's two against one then,' says Pom bravely.

恶霸猫不是他们的对手。"干得漂亮，乒乒！"
"你也是，乒乒！"

The bully-cat cannot be against this. 'Well done, Pom!'
'You too, Pim!'

"下来吧，天眼，"乒乒和乓乓喊道，"警报解除。"
"谢谢你们，乒乒和乓乓。你们是真正的大英雄！"

'You can come down Sky-Eyes,' shout Pim and Pom. 'The coast is clear.'
'Thank you Pim and Pom. You are true heroes!'

第二天……

"我们上报啦！我们登上报纸啦！"

And the next day...
'We're in it. We're in the newspaper!'

"猫咪乒乓和乒乓勇救暹罗猫。"

'Brave cats Pim and Pom save Siamese.'

猫咪乒乓和乓乓勇救暹罗猫